PIERRE'S NOT THERE

URSULA DUBOSARSKY

With illustrations by
CHRISTOPHER NIELSEN

ALLEN&UNWIN
SYDNEY・MELBOURNE・AUCKLAND・LONDON

First published by Allen & Unwin in 2020

Copyright © Text, Ursula Dubosarsky 2020
Copyright © Illustrations, Christopher Nielsen 2020

All rights reserved. No part of this book may be reproduced or transmitted in any form or by any means, electronic or mechanical, including photocopying, recording or by any information storage and retrieval system, without prior permission in writing from the publisher. The Australian *Copyright Act 1968* (the Act) allows a maximum of one chapter or ten per cent of this book, whichever is the greater, to be photocopied by any educational institution for its educational purposes provided that the educational institution (or body that administers it) has given a remuneration notice to the Copyright Agency (Australia) under the Act.

Allen & Unwin
83 Alexander Street
Crows Nest NSW 2065
Australia
Phone: (61 2) 8425 0100
Email: info@allenandunwin.com
Web: www.allenandunwin.com

A catalogue record for this book is available from the National Library of Australia

ISBN 978 1 76052 593 4

For teaching resources, explore www.allenandunwin.com/resources/for-teachers

Cover and text design by Romina Edwards
Set in 11/20 pt FoundryWilson
Printed in August 2020 by McPherson's Printing Group, Australia

10 9 8 7 6 5 4 3 2 1

The paper in this book is FSC® certified. FSC® promotes environmentally responsible, socially beneficial and economically viable management of the world's forests.

www.ursuladubosarsky.squarespace.com
www.childrenslaureate.org.au
www.chrisillo.com

*For Jan Preston and Mike Webb-Pullman,
true friends who saved the day x*
UD

*For Suzanne, who takes my hand
and leads me to the river*
CN

CAST
(in order of appearance)

LARA

MOTHER

PIERRE

OLD HORSE

MR PUNCH

ZADY

BEAR-KING

Chapter ONE

Lara had always wished she was a dog, and one day, just for a short time, she actually became one.

This is how it happened.

It was on a day when Lara was going with her mother to work, because it was the school holidays. They had to get up very early in the pale morning to take first the bus, then the long train journey along the snaking tracks while the engine buzzed and the train stopped and started again at station after station. Lara thought it would never end. Finally they burst, the two of them, out of the train, down the escalator and into the dazzling wideness of Circular Quay and the row of wharves with ferries moving in and out like slow dancers across the glassy harbour.

Lara breathed in the salty air and the sunshine burned her throat and she felt like she was floating. Flying! Now the sky was blue, not white, and the air was warm and would only become warmer.

'Quickly,' said Lara's mother, 'and we'll just make it.'

So they rushed through the turnstiles, their bags bouncing, hanging onto their hats, down to where their ferry was waiting impatiently, pulling on its mooring.

Lara and her mother crossed the gangplank onto the ferry. Lara wanted to run up and across the curving metal bridge by herself, but her mother held her hand tightly in case she fell over into the waves below. It was impossible, as the barrier on either side of the gangplank was too high, unless Lara took it into her head to dive over the edge. She didn't mind her mother's grasp. She liked the feel of the familiar fingers wrapped around her own, like a rope she could hold onto and use to pull herself upwards, out of the depths, if she had to.

The deckhand shouted, trundled in the gangplank and a horn blew a long whinnying cry. The ferry broke loose from the wharf and pushed out onto the waves and as the ground moved beneath her, Lara felt as if she was heading into another world.

The muddle of passengers dashed to find seats, indoors, out on the deck, up the stairs. Lara felt something stab her inside as she saw her mother heading for one of the indoor seats.

'Can't we sit outside?' she cried. 'Please!'

She couldn't bear to be stuck in the stuffy grey room with the small windows and the heat and hum of the motor. She had to be outside – to be free!

'Yes, all right,' said Lara's mother. She had already taken out her book from her bag, ready to sit and read. 'Off you go, then, and find us a spot.'

Lara ran out onto the deck. The ferry was crowded because of the holidays and the benches were full of knees and ankles and baskets and bags and big hats and the smell of sunscreen lotion and the fizz of cans being opened and laughter and complaints and sunglasses and towels and small children and smaller babies and a very old lady with a thick walking stick and a veil and a smell as sweet as fairy floss. Lara picked her way in and out of it all, hopping, jumping and springing as lightly as she could, like trying not to step on flowerbeds in a garden.

'Sorry,' she said, several times over. 'Sorry, sorry,' until there was a gap and she leaped through and found a slice of a bench right at the front of the boat where nobody was. Her mother, following her, slid down to sit on it and held her book on her lap for a moment, then breathed in deeply.

Lara flung herself up to the arrowhead of the boat, the furthest tip of the ferry. How lucky that she was the first one, the only one, there! She leaned over as far as she could and felt the faint splash of spray on her cheeks as the waves around her rose in jagged peaks that disappeared as quickly as they were formed.

The ferry pushed onwards between the jutting green headlands. Her mother calmly read her book as the ferry churned on. Lara stood watching the land pass and the ocean broaden, in a kind of trance. Seagulls sailed in the sky above, catching drifts of wind, swooping down to the water's surface and up again with their mysterious cries.

Lara looked down into the dark green water below, scudding past. There would be sharks down there, and stingrays. Forests of seaweed. She could swim, of course she could, but this would not be like a swimming pool or even the beach where you could retreat to the sand if the waves were too high. Still – to be able to be somewhere else, deep in the ocean, somewhere where nothing was familiar or known, where you could even become someone else ...

She felt a thumping at her feet, coming through the floorboards.

'Oh!' said Lara.

In front of her, in the dark space under the tip of the boat, half-hidden in shadow, was a dog. It lay paws stretched out like a stone lion at the gateway of a palace. Its head was huge and so were its haunches; its fur was thick and rough. The dog gazed at Lara, its eyes yellow like honey in the sunlight. It wagged its big heavy tail, *thump thump*, on the ground.

Lara, who loved all dogs, knelt down and held out her hand towards it, as she had been taught to do with animals she didn't know.

'Hello, dog,' she said.

The dog blinked. Its eyelids were thick velvety

curtains. Slowly, with consideration, it licked Lara's fingers.

'Good dog,' she said. 'What's your name, then?'

Gently, she felt under the matted fur of its neck for a collar and tag. There was no collar.

'Are you a ship dog?' said Lara. 'Do you belong to the captain?'

The dog opened its mouth and let its great tongue hang across the row of shiny teeth on its bottom jaw.

'I bet you would be a good swimmer,' she

murmured. The dog turned its head slightly, listening, its black ears pricking up. 'If you fell into the water, you wouldn't be afraid.'

Dogs could swim without being taught. She sighed, remembering the weeks of swimming lessons she had done, all the kicking and breathing practice, *one, two, three, breathe! One, two, three, breathe!* Dogs, though, knew exactly what to do, and nobody had to show them. They swam valiantly, with their heads above the water, their four legs churning below, the bubbles rising to the surface.

'I wish I could swim like you, without having to learn,' she said, closing her eyes, and everything around her became silent and invisible. 'I wish I was free, from school, from swimming lessons, from everything, like a dog.'

The ferry's engine changed gear, the speed of the boat dropped and a bell rang. The land became larger and closer, and Lara, opening her eyes, could see the leaves on the trees and birds on the branches. The brilliant white furrow beside the boat turned to soft foam. People called out to each other, babies cried. Her mother closed her book and put it back in her bag and stood up, ready to go, holding one hand to her forehead to shield her eyes against the sun. The ferry swung in towards the waiting wharf.

The dog also got up and shook itself, stretching its huge legs.

'Time to go,' said Lara, kindly, to the dog. 'Your owner will come and find you now.'

She stroked the top of its head, and the dog made a rumbling sound, not a growl, more like a purr.

'Come on, Lara!' said her mother.

The deck was a huddle of moving people, eager to get off. The ferry swayed to and fro as it came to rest and the load of passengers – friends, family, strangers – were pushed, laughing, even screaming, grabbing onto each other as the grey wooden wharf posts, covered with seaweed and mussels, creaked and shuddered.

Lara turned for one last glimpse of the black dog. But it had already gone.

Chapter TWO

Lara and her mother stepped across the gangplank, back onto dry land.

'Steady!' called the deckhand, grinning to the queue of pushing passengers. 'Wait a bit, and we'll all get off.'

In front of the wharf was a long, green park with thick grass and tall Norfolk pines with drooping dark-green branches. Beyond the edge of the grass was a smear of a beach with white sand, sparkling like glitter. It was a place where people came for the day, to picnic, to play, to swim or to walk through the bush that grew in tangles along the coast.

'Afterwards,' said her mother, 'we'll have our lunch on the beach and you can have a swim.'

In her mother's string bag, Lara knew, were towels, swimsuits, sandwiches, bananas and a bottle of lemonade that had been in the freezer all night. Usually her mother would pack some slices of cake as well, and the fact that she didn't this time made Lara suspect that she might be planning on buying them an ice cream from the kiosk next to the big fish and chip shop, where already – at half past nine! – there was a line of customers and Lara could smell the fat and the salt and the fish being parcelled up

and handed over the counter. There was a giant ice cream cone painted on the wall, dripping multi-coloured flavours of gelato ...

With the crowd, they walked up the sandstone path that led through the middle of the park. Along the way people dropped off in little groups, like bits of loose gravel, and they spread out rugs and lay down on the grass, or tore off their clothes ready to swim, or began kicking a ball. Lara was overcome with a need to run – she just had to run – and she took off, upwards, holding her arms out as far as they could go on either side.

'Watch where you're going!' came her mother's voice behind her, with the calm tapping of her heels on the pathway. 'There's no hurry.'

There *was* a hurry – there was! It was like the bursting feeling she had when the teacher handed out the paintbrushes at school and she was afraid there wouldn't be enough, or the stampede of children when the bell rang for lunch, as though the playground might disappear if they didn't get there in time. She ran and ran, arms outstretched, through the trees, like a seagull in full flight.

She stopped, panting, at the low stone wall where the park ended and the street began, and waited for her mother. The park was dappled with morning shadows. Something loped in and out of the pines, their trunks as straight as fence posts, winding its way back and forth.

It was the big black dog from the ferry! Where was its owner then? There was nobody walking in front or behind with a lead, or tossing a stick, or calling for it to follow. Had it got off the ferry all by itself? It didn't look at all like a stray dog, lost and lonely. This was a free dog ...

Lara's mother reached the top of the park, just as the dog ran away through the trees.

'What are you staring at, Lara?' her mother asked, smiling quizzically.

'Only a dog,' said Lara. 'The dog that was on the ferry.'

'Ah, a dog,' said her mother. 'Let's cross the road.'

There was a row of houses in front of them facing the ocean. Lara knew which one they were going to without being told because her mother had often described it to her. It was built of mulberry brick, with a sloping slate roof that was grey with salt and green with moss. The white window frames curled like cream on a birthday cake, and there was a chimney on the roof, and the clouds floated above it like puffs of smoke.

At the peak of the roof a flag flapped and cracked in the gusts of sea wind. It was faded and torn and had a picture of a big brown bear on it on all fours, and behind the bear was a swirl of golden stars.

'What country is that?' wondered Lara.

Her mother laughed.

'No country I've ever heard of,' she said.

They walked in the front gate. Garden beds on either side of the pathway leading to the door were filled with rosebushes thick with flowers, red and yellow like flames. Lara's mother knelt down in the earth next to one of the rosebushes. Lara knew what she was searching for – the key. There were all sorts of places that people left their keys hidden when they weren't at home. In their gardens, or in pots, or even in passageways full of spiders.

Her mother carefully pushed apart the thorny rose stems, until she found a little blue pot between the lacy roots and decaying petals. She slipped her fingers into it and extracted a key, then got back on her feet, dusting her knees. She fitted the key into the lock of the front door and gave it a couple of twists. She took it out, pushed it in harder and twisted it again.

'There's a trick to it,' she muttered. 'It always takes a bit of a turn, this way and that.'

The house doesn't want us to come in, thought Lara. *It wants us to go away.*

But she was wrong. The lock gave way and the door opened wide.

Chapter THREE

The sudden coolness of indoors washed over them both as they stepped inside. The house smelled of sugar and shiny shoes. The floor under their feet was made of hundreds of little blue and yellow tiles, patterned like a carpet, and the walls were silky and the colour of ice, like the walls of an igloo.

'That's better,' said her mother, taking off her hat in relief. 'Sooner indoors than out on a day like today.'

She closed the door firmly behind them and hung up her hat on a hook. She left the door key in a little dish painted with green leaves that was on a narrow hall table with an oval mirror, slightly too high for Lara to catch sight of her face.

'Right then,' said Lara's mother.

'Right then' meant that her mind was already busy and intent on the task at hand. She bustled off briskly, putting on her apron. Lara knew how the morning would be spent. First the dusting, then the sweeping, then vacuuming, then tidying and folding, then finally, just before leaving, mopping the floors. Lara would have liked to help, but her mother wouldn't let her. She wasn't allowed to touch anything, do anything. 'Keep out of the way, be quiet and be careful,' her mother said, 'find a chair and read a book, or go out into the garden. And don't bother me, I'll be busy.'

Lara stood for a moment in the hallway, listening to the opening and closing of cupboards, the clatter of things being taken out and put back in again. *Thud!* Her mother was dislodging spider webs with the end of a broom.

On the hallway table there was a crimson pot plant of the tiniest tree Lara had ever seen. It was just like a real pine tree, with a trunk and branches and pine leaves, yet the whole plant was no taller than the width of her hand. Underneath it sat a cross-legged clay figure of a smiling bearded man in a cap with a tiny bell on the end of it. He had something in his hand. What was it – a stick? A whip? Lara peered even closer until the little man and his face became larger. He wasn't smiling, he was snarling.

She stepped back and went quickly down the hallway, to get away from the angry little man. She passed two closed doors and then arrived at a big, open living room. The sofa was covered with cushions, silver and gold, like a pile of pebbles in a stream. Everything seemed very clean, too clean even to touch. She wondered about the people who lived in the house. Did they have children? It didn't seem the sort of house that would have children, or at least not anymore ...

She could see the backyard through the low window of the living room. She walked through the kitchen with its glistening floor, its massive fridge and sparkling sinks, to find the back door. It didn't need a key to open – just a simple latch.

Outside again the sun was bright and burning like a lit match and the singing of cicadas drowned out the rolling hum of the ocean. Lara jumped down the back steps onto the square lawn. In one corner there was a blooming frangipani tree, branches groping in all directions. That was all. There were no other plants or flowers. The garden was enclosed by a grey wooden fence, too high for a person standing to see over. In the middle of the lawn was a still fountain of caramel stone, surrounded by a pool of water.

I wonder if it's a fishpond, thought Lara.

She walked towards it. A blanket of humidity fell over her. The yellow grass crackled under her feet. She knelt down next to the fountain and peered into the pond. It was murky with weeds. She picked up a stray twig from the ground and stirred the surface. No fish – they wouldn't be able to breathe in there. Nothing could live in there except slime. She let the twig drop into the water and watched it sink slowly down, like a dying leaf.

In the centre of the pool was a dry metal spout coming out of the mouth of a stone fish. That would be where the water would gush out, when the fountain was working. There must be a button somewhere to push that would make it flow. Imagine what her mother would say if she did something like that ...

Crack!

Something came skidding against the side of the fountain where she was standing. For a moment she thought it was some sort of insect – a bee? – but then she realised it was a glass marble, coloured yellow and black. It rolled across the ground to her feet and came to a stop. She picked it up, frowning. Where on earth had that come from? Could a bird have dropped it? Magpies, she knew, picked up all sorts of odd things when they were building their nests.

She twisted around. There was no sign of a bird. Everything in the garden was still and the only sound was the throbbing chants of the cicadas.

Then her eyes ran up the back of the house and saw that one of the very top windows was open. And leaning out the window was a boy about her own age, in a red jacket. He was smiling at her.

Chapter FOUR

Her mother had said the house was empty! That nobody was home. That's why she had to fish the key out of the little blue pot at the front to let them in.

If nobody was home, who was that boy at the window?

Of course, Lara should have simply gone straightaway and told her mother that there was a boy upstairs. But she didn't. She didn't know why. She left the dry fountain and its dark pond, and ran across the lawn, up the steps, through the back door of the kitchen. It slammed behind her in a rush of hot wind.

She ran down the hallway to the bottom of the staircase. Hanging onto the glossy white banister, she took the carpeted steps up two at a time. At the top, there was a closed door with a round brass handle.

He's in there, she thought. Should she knock? 'Hello?' she called out.

She paused a moment. There was no answer. No sound of footsteps, nothing. She knocked. The knock sounded hollow and musical, like tapping on a half-filled bottle of water. Still nothing.

She tightened her fingers around the doorknob and pushed the door open. It was dark. The shutters of the windows were drawn. It was like twilight. She stepped into the room. She could hear her mother with the vacuum cleaner humming and buzzing, up and down, louder and softer, like a muffled bee. Buzzing and humming, humming and buzzing ...

'Hello,' said a voice.

She saw his hands first, two hands held up in the half-dark, all ten fingers.

'You're here!' he said.

Now she was more used to the darkness, his shape became clearer, as though someone was drawing in the details of his face, his body. It was the boy at the window. He came up closer. His eyes were large and brown.

'Well, yes, I'm here,' she agreed. 'Who are you?'

'It's me,' he said. 'It's me. I'm Pierre.'

'Hello,' said Lara, still cautious. 'I'm Lara.'

The two children stood in the middle of the room, watching each other.

'I saw you from the garden,' said Lara.

'Yes!' said the boy. 'And I saw you from my window.'

'You threw a marble at me,' accused Lara.

'I wanted to get your attention,' said Pierre. 'I'm a good shot. I knew I wouldn't hit you.'

'You could have called out,' Lara said. 'You still could have hurt me. Or broken something.'

Pierre dropped his hands to either side of his body, and then put them in his pockets and said nothing. His jacket was almost like a uniform, with tassels on the shoulders and shining brass buttons on the cuffs.

'What are you doing here?' she asked.

Pierre put his head to one side.

'I live here, of course,' he said.

'My mother said nobody was at home.'

'Is that your mother?' he said. 'Down the stairs?'

'Well, yes,' said Lara. 'She's cleaning the house. So that's why I'm here. You should come downstairs and say hello to her. She thinks there's nobody at home.'

'I can't!' said Pierre at once, and he sounded stricken with panic.

Lara was baffled. 'Why not?'

Pierre didn't answer. Lara surveyed the room. Against one wall there was a bed and a shelf. Next to it was a rug with a pile of books and toy cars on it.

'Is this your bedroom?' she asked. 'Can we open the shutters? It's so dark in here.'

'It has to be dark,' said Pierre. 'I'm putting on a show.'

'A show?'

'A puppet show!' said Pierre. 'Come and see!'

Eagerly, he took hold of her arm, and drew her to the furthest corner of the room. A narrow shaft of light shone through a gap in the window shutter like a spotlight.

'Oh!' cried Lara, falling on her knees.

It was a puppet theatre! Made of wood, painted with curls and columns in faded gold and silver, like a temple from ancient Greece. At the front there were two velvet curtains and behind them a sheet of scenery gleamed in the darkness, snow on top of a mountain.

'It's amazing!' breathed Lara, entranced. 'It's so beautiful! Where did it come from?'

'It's my grandmother's,' said Pierre.

'It's old,' said Lara.

'It's very old,' agreed Pierre. 'Very, very old.' He waved his arms around dramatically. 'Maybe hundreds of years old!' He paused and added, 'It's magic.'

'A puppet show isn't magic,' said Lara. 'It's a puppet show.'

'This one *is* magic,' insisted Pierre.

'How?'

Pierre shook his head.

'It's magic, that's all,' he said.

It was exactly as anyone would imagine a perfect puppet theatre to be. The only other real puppet theatre Lara had ever seen had been a Punch and Judy show, down at the pavilion near the beach one summer. That had been big, tall enough for adults to stand behind. This theatre, though, was especially made for children. Just the right size.

She raised her hand to the red curtains and drew her fingertips across them. The material moved under her fingers as if it was alive, softer than a cat.

Chapter FIVE

'Have you got any puppets?' Lara asked.

Pierre jumped up at once.

'I'll show you!' he said.

He ran back to his bed and hauled out from under it a brown, dusty and battered suitcase and dragged it over. He lifted up the lid and let it fall back. It was full of puppets, piled on top of each other, a jumble of faces, their arms and legs poking wildly up in all directions. Lara's eyes opened wide.

'Can I touch them?'

'Yes, of course. That's what they're for.'

Pierre was watching her with an excited, hopeful expression. She lifted up the puppet that was near the top of the pile. It was a girl in a dress covered with stars and long hair made out of brown wool and a little crown on her head. *A princess*, thought Lara. She put her back in the pile and dug in and found another, a soldier with a gun on his shoulder, and a crisscrossed striped uniform. She dug deeper. She tugged on something and there was a little jingling sound. She tugged a bit more.

'A horse!'

It was a horse with big eyes, and a tangled bridle and reins, with little bells attached. She laid it down and picked up a boy with a red coat and a strange smiling face.

'He looks like you,' she said, laughing, to Pierre.

'Does he?' said Pierre.

'Yes,' said Lara. 'I wonder what story he's from?'

'What do you mean?'

'You know, the play, the story.' She waved at the other puppets in the suitcase. 'They're all characters in a story. Aren't they?'

'Oh!' said Pierre. His face was very near hers and his eyes were wet like raindrops. 'A story,' he breathed.

'Yes,' said Lara, putting the puppet down again.

'Can I tell you a story?'

'Sure,' said Lara, shrugging. 'I'm listening.'

'Well,' began Pierre. Then he stopped. 'It's a hard story. It's about me.'

'So it's a true story,' said Lara.

'Yes,' said Pierre. 'It's about when I used to live in a very nice house and I had seven big brothers and sisters and a very nice mother and father—'

He stopped again.

'Go on,' said Lara.

'One night, a pack of wolves broke into the house and ate them all!' The words came bolting out of Pierre's mouth.

For a moment, Lara was silent.

'Did you say ... a pack of wolves ate your family?'

'Yes,' said Pierre.

'Your whole family?'

'Everyone except me,' said Pierre.

Lara did not believe a word of it.

'Why didn't they eat you?'

'I was the smallest and the youngest, you see,' said Pierre, 'but I also happen to have excellent hearing and I heard the wolves outside the door and I told my brothers and sisters and my mother and father there was something bad out there, but they didn't believe me, and then it was too late, and the wolves came in and I ran to the deepest, darkest corner and because I was so small they didn't see me.'

'*You* saw *them*,' said Lara.

'Yes,' said Pierre. 'I saw them. A big pack of wolves. There were so many I couldn't count them. I was so frightened.' He turned very pale. 'I waited and waited until everything was quiet again and all the wolves had gone. Then I came out, and it was dreadful; the wolves had eaten everyone up. Not just my brothers and sisters and my very nice mother and father,' said Pierre, 'but they ate all the food as well and all the plates and the knives and forks and cups and saucers. Everything.'

Lara, who knew the story must be made up, still found herself asking: 'So what did you do then?'

'I cried,' said Pierre, simply. 'I cried and cried, because I did love all my brothers and sisters, and my mother and father, you see. And then I remembered that my mother told me that if I ever needed help and there was nobody left, I should leave the house and go and find my grandmother. So I ran away as fast as I could.'

'To find your grandmother,' said Lara.

'Exactly,' said Pierre.

'Where does your grandmother live?'

'That is the problem,' said Pierre with a sigh. 'I don't know where she lives. All my mother told me was that she lived on the other side of the river.'

'What river?'

'I don't know,' said Pierre. 'I wish I had asked her. Now it's too late.'

'So,' said Lara, 'you're stuck.'

'I knew you would understand!' said Pierre, seizing both of Lara's hands. 'I knew you would know! That's why I threw my marble at you, to make you come and see!'

He scrambled up from the floor.

'Stay there! Sit in front of the theatre,' he ordered. 'I'll show you. I'll show you what happens every time. Every single time!'

He skipped over to the window and snapped the shutters completely shut. The room went black, with not even an edge of daylight coming in the cracks. Then he ran back and switched on a reading light that was on the floor at the foot of the stage.

Lara sat cross-legged in front of the theatre. The golden paint glowed and the little velvet curtains trembled. She heard a car outside on the street slow down and then speed away.

Pierre called out: 'Ladies and gentlemen, is everyone ready? The show is about to begin!'

And in a great swoosh the curtains flew apart.

Chapter SIX

The stage was empty. In the background was the painted scene of snow-topped hills, with clumps of flat sheep and flat yellow flowers on the slopes. The sky above the hills was pale blue, with one mild cloud. The light from below shone on the dusty air and it glittered.

Up sprang a puppet. It was the boy puppet in the red jacket, the puppet that looked like Pierre. He bowed deeply. Lara clapped. Of course, she was the only one clapping, but the clatter echoed around the room as if it was full of hands.

'Thank you, thank you,' said the puppet in Pierre's voice. 'Thank you so much.'

The boy puppet bobbed up and down in front of the mountains, humming. Lara knew from the puppet show she'd seen at the beach that it wasn't like an ordinary play, where you had to sit silently and listen. You could shout anything at puppets, and they would hear you and answer. So she called out:

'Who are you?'

The boy puppet stopped humming. 'Who am I?' The puppet scratched his head, and smiled with his sewn-on smile. 'I'm Pierre!'

'Hallo Pierre!' said Lara.

Pierre sang:

'I am Pierre, I am Pierre,
I am Pierre but Pierre's not there!'

Lara uncrossed her legs and sat up on her knees.

'What are you doing, Pierre?'

'I'm running,' said Pierre. 'I am running over the hills. Running and running. See me running!'

He bounced with a funny up-and-down movement, as though he was riding a horse, up and down the stage and back again.

'Where are you running to, Pierre?' Lara called out.

'I am very far away, far from my home,' replied Pierre. 'I am running to find my grandmother.

That's where I'm going.' He came to a halt, aghast. 'But I think I am lost. Yes, I'm lost!' He put his head in his funny puppet hands. 'Oh no! I am lost!'

The curtain closed with an abrupt slap.

Pierre came out on all fours from behind the theatre, holding the boy puppet to his chest.

'That's it?' said Lara. 'That's the end?'

'That's it,' he said, in a miserable voice. 'This is my problem, you see.'

Lara shook her head. 'I don't understand.'

'Every time I start the play,' said Pierre, flopping down on his back on the floor, 'I get stuck. I'm always stuck, just at that point. The same thing, over and over again. I stand in the middle of the stage and nothing happens. I don't know where my grandmother is, I'm all alone and I don't know how to get there.'

Pierre put his puppet up in the air above him. The two Pierres stared at each other. He glanced at Lara, sideways, from underneath his eyelids.

'That's why I thought, when I saw you, down at the fountain ... that's why I thought maybe – I thought – that you could help me.'

'Me?'

'Yes. When I saw you, I had a feeling about you.'

'What sort of feeling?' asked Lara.

'I don't know ...' replied Pierre. 'I had a feeling – that—'

Lara waited.

'That you would be good at pretending to be someone else. That ... that ... you could make up a story for me, for my puppet show.'

'You mean, if I was one of the other puppets?'

'Yes!' said Pierre, sitting up straight. 'That's exactly what I mean! Will you? Please?'

'Only then there won't be an audience,' Lara pointed out. 'If I'm not there.'

'We don't need an audience!' Pierre declared. He spun around on the spot with excitement. 'Our play will be just for us!'

Lara shuffled over on her knees to the brown suitcase full of puppets. 'Who should I be?'

'You choose!' said Pierre. 'Whichever one you like! Put one on, and then come and join me!'

He disappeared again around the back of the puppet theatre. Lara sat in front of the higgledy-piggledy pile in the suitcase. Which would she pick? It was so dark she could hardly see which one was which.

'Come on! Hurry up!' shouted Pierre from behind the theatre.

Lara plunged her arm into the suitcase, as if it was a lucky dip. Her fingers searched around in the muddle of cloth and hard-nobbled surfaces, wool, buttons and thick painted faces. Which one, which one? Finally her hand slipped inside a glove and she groped for the space at its neck where she could put her two biggest fingers. There!

She pushed her thumb into one of the front arms and her little finger and fourth finger into the other. She brought it out, and turned it towards her in the shimmering half-dark. All she could see were two bright glinting eyes.

Chapter SEVEN

Lara crawled on her hands and knees with the puppet to the back of the theatre. The space behind was much smaller than she had thought, only enough room for her and Pierre with their shoulders bumping each other. And there was no beautiful gold and silver swirling paint, just splintery dull wood and the back of the red curtain was a rough brown hessian. But that sudden wild feeling! She had such a wild feeling! *Anything can happen here*, thought Lara. *Anything.*

She was ready with the puppet. Her fingers were

tingling and her heart was beating very fast.

'Ready?' whispered Pierre right in her ear.

He leaned over and tugged a string on one side of the stage that operated the curtains. There was a gush of light as the two halves parted. For a moment Lara's eyes were blinded. She blinked, several times. It was dark again, then faintly light.

'WHO'S THERE?' a voice boomed out. Was that Pierre? He sounded so far away and he was right next to her. And yet—

'Who is it? Come out at once!'

Pierre wasn't next to her. He'd gone. There was nobody. It was all so dark and dusty. She sneezed. Had he gone to the front to sit and watch? Was he playing a trick on her?

When she tried, she couldn't reach her neck around the side of the theatre to see if she could spot him. The space that had been so cramped had become suddenly large. What had happened? She swung her head upwards to the ceiling. It had disappeared into nothingness. There was a strong smell of sawdust and something else – turpentine.

Where was Pierre? Pierre was nowhere. *Pierre, Pierre, Pierre's not there.*

She stood up and moved slowly, feeling her way. She felt heavy and closed in, like being in a thick forest. Except instead of trees, she was pushing her way through layers of thin panels of wood, packed together on either side of her, like a series of sliding doors. They were tilting, backwards and forwards, as though they were about to fall over.

She peered into the cracks between the panels. Each one was a giant painting. There was a sandy desert with clumps of cactus; there was a dungeon with one tiny window and chains on the wall; there was a graveyard at night with the moon rising above the tombs; there was a grand ballroom with a hanging chandelier and palm trees in pots; there was a garden; there was a high tower; there was a castle moat; there was a forest.

The paint of the forest was still wet. That was the strong smell! Wet paint ... Lara felt dizzy. For a

moment she thought she was going to faint. It was as though she had stepped right into somebody else's mind.

'What happened to my sandals?' she wondered out loud, because she realised she could feel the ground underneath her, lots of little sharp stones and loose earth.

'Who's there?' came the voice again.

She licked her lips, felt a row of very sharp teeth, top and bottom. She closed her mouth and felt the crunch of her jaw.

'Please? Who is it?'

It *was* Pierre. Light shone above him, brighter every moment.

'Pierre!' She sprang to him in relief. 'Where are we? What's happened?'

'Don't hurt me!' cried Pierre, shielding his face with both hands.

'Hurt you? Why would I hurt you?' said Lara. 'It's me, Lara!'

She breathed in and out, sniffing the air.

Something, *someone* was purring, like a cat. A very big cat. No, not purring. It was much deeper, growling ...

It's me! thought Lara. *The growling is me!*

Pierre's round eyes were filled with fear.

'Lara – you're a WOLF!'

Chapter EIGHT

A hundred lightning bolts leaped inside her, all shooting in different directions.

'I'm—' Lara stammered. 'I'm—'

She stopped. She looked down at herself in slow astonishment. Her sandals had gone, and so had her clothes. Instead of her shorts and shirt there was something thick and coarse clinging to her arms and legs. Fur. Instead of feet and hands she had paws. Four wide paws with curving silver claws.

'I—'

She turned her head, to see what she knew must

be there. She could feel the weight of it. She had a tail – her own tail! Hanging down like a huge paintbrush, nearly touching the ground.

'What—' she said. 'I—'

Lara's ears pricked up, hearing everything as though it was ten times louder than usual. Through her wet black nose every smell was a hundred times stronger.

'You've turned into a wolf,' said Pierre. 'You've turned into a wolf!'

A wolf? How could she be a wolf? Wolves were fierce, they lived in packs. They howled at the moon and people were afraid of them. Lara paced back and forth, back and forth, her head hanging down, feeling the ground with the pads of her paws. A wolf—

'I'm not a wolf!' she said, turning suddenly, quite sure. 'I'm a dog!'

'A dog?' said Pierre, faltering. 'You *look* like a wolf to me!'

'I'm not a wolf,' said Lara. 'I know I'm not.

Definitely. I can feel it, inside me.'

She could feel her dog's heart and her dog's blood beating through it.

'Please believe me, Pierre,' she said, padding up to him. 'I'm not a wolf. I'm a dog. I won't hurt you.'

She wagged her great tail, just a little.

'I'm afraid,' whispered Pierre. 'You might eat me up.'

'I won't,' said Lara. 'I don't want to. I want to be your friend. Like a dog.'

Pierre took a step back, and then another.

'I want to help you,' said Lara.

'How can you help me?'

'I will help you find your grandmother,' said Lara.

Pierre was silent. Then he said, and his voice sounded so sad and so hopeful: 'Do *you* know where my grandmother lives?'

'Well,' said Lara. 'If I'm a dog – and I *am* a dog – even though I don't know why or how – that's the sort of thing dogs can do. They find people. You know, people who are lost in the bush, or the snow.

Dogs find them, wherever they are.'

Mysteriously, while they had been talking, the air had turned a luminous orange-pink. Lara lifted her front paw and held her head very still.

'What's happening?' said Pierre.

'I don't know,' said Lara.

A forest rose up around them, thick with leaves and branches. There was a smell of smoke.

'We must leave, Pierre,' said Lara. 'Straightaway. I can feel danger.'

'Yes,' said Pierre. 'So can I.'

'Will you trust me?' asked Lara.

'I – if you promise not to get too close,' said Pierre.

'I promise,' said Lara.

'And that you won't eat me – or anyone else,' he added quickly.

'I don't want to eat anyone,' said Lara. 'You will see.'

Pierre held out his hand, and put it very lightly and carefully on her back. She felt his trembling fingers through her fur.

'Then let's go,' he said.

The Curtain Rises

SCENE ONE

THE FOREST

PIERRE *and* LARA *enter the forest together. There are uncanny noises – birds, insects, swooping wings. A half-moon rises above the tallest tree.*

PIERRE   Lara?

LARA   (*not turning her head, always alert*)
              Yes, Pierre?

PIERRE   Do you know where we're going?

LARA   To find your grandmother,
             of course.

PIERRE   Well, yes, I know, but – do you
             know where we are? We have been
             walking for such a long time now.
             Hours and hours.

LARA   It doesn't matter where we are,
             Pierre. It matters what direction
             we're heading. And we're heading
             for your grandmother.

PIERRE   How do you know which way to go?

LARA   Shhh. I'm following a scent.

She lowers her nose to the ground, sniffing.

PIERRE   A what?

LARA   (*importantly*) A scent – a smell.
             A trail.

PIERRE   You've never even met my grandmother! How do you know what she smells like?

LARA   Shhh! I'm concentrating. (*Anxiously, to herself*) I must be able to smell *something*. I'm a dog, after all.

PIERRE   Can we stop here for a little while, for a rest, Lara? After you've finished sniffing?

LARA   It's too cold to stop. We have to keep going to stay warm.

PIERRE   Just for a few minutes. Please, Lara! My feet are so sore.

LARA   And what about me? I've got four feet to get sore, remember, not two.

PIERRE   Please, Lara!

LARA	(*sighing*) Yes, all right. We could rest under this tree for a little while. And if we lean up close to each other, we'll keep each other warm.

LARA *lies herself down in a hollow of the big tree roots.* PIERRE *hesitates.*

LARA	Come on, Pierre. You're the one that wanted to stop. You can't stand there by yourself. It's freezing.
PIERRE	Are you sure you're not a wolf?
LARA	I'm not a wolf, I keep telling you!

Reluctantly, PIERRE *sits down close to* LARA.

PIERRE	Your heart is beating very loudly, Lara.
LARA	That's because I'm a dog. Dogs have big hearts.

They sit silently together. PIERRE *falls asleep, and begins to snore.* LARA's *eyes droop, but she does not quite fall asleep. Her attention is attracted by something in the distance. She gets up, alert. There is faint flickering light in the distance. She pushes sleeping* PIERRE *with her nose.*

LARA   Pierre! Wake up!

PIERRE   (*rubbing his eyes*) What?

LARA   Something's coming!

The flickering light is coming closer to them, down the forest path.

PIERRE   (*jumping up and clutching* LARA's *fur*) What is it?

There is the sound of squeaking wheels. Finally an OLD HORSE *drawing a tumbledown cart, with a rocking lantern tied to one side, enters the stage.*

The OLD HORSE *is very thin and the colour of snow, like a ghost. His eyes are shielded with leather hoods. Sitting hunched at the driver's seat of the cart with the reins in his hands is* MR PUNCH. *He is wearing a long, curling hat and has a ragged grey beard. When* MR PUNCH *sees* PIERRE *and* LARA, *he pulls hard on the reins, and the* OLD HORSE *comes to a solid stop.*

MR PUNCH (*very cheerfully*) Well, well, isn't this a nice surprise?

LARA Grrrrrrrrrrrrrrrrrrrrrrrrrrr!

PIERRE (*cautiously*) Hello.

MR PUNCH *jumps down from the cart and stretches his long legs and arms.*

MR PUNCH I'm going to give the horse a rest for a few minutes. You know horses, always complaining.

He smacks the OLD HORSE *on the back. The* OLD HORSE *stamps his hooves, raising a cloud of dust and making the ground shake.* PIERRE *nearly falls over.* MR PUNCH *goes to the back of the cart and takes out a bottle of water, gulping it down in great mouthfuls. The water spills over his face.*

MR PUNCH (*offering the bottle to* PIERRE)
Want a drink?

PIERRE Well – I – actually, I think your horse is thirsty. You should give him some first.

The OLD HORSE *is looking longingly at the water bottle.* MR PUNCH *puts the lid back on and tosses the bottle back into the cart.*

MR PUNCH I've come a long way today, and I've got a long way to go. Can't be wasting water on an animal, can I?

	(*Pauses.*) And what about yourself, young man? Where are you off to?
LARA	(*warningly*) Grrrrrrrrrr!

The OLD HORSE *stamps again.*

PIERRE	Is your horse all right? It's like he's trying to say something.
MR PUNCH	(*cackling*) You're right! How clever you are! In fact, he's saying, 'Hit me on the head!'

MR PUNCH *whips a club from his pocket and raises it in the air.* PIERRE *is horrified.* LARA *leaps forwards with a menacing growl.*

LARA	Grrrrrrrrrrrrrrrrrr!
PIERRE	Don't hit him! You mustn't hit him!

MR PUNCH (*lowering the club*) I wouldn't hit him. Why would I do that? (*He casts a malevolent glance at* LARA.) Is that a wolf? I wouldn't be travelling around with a wolf, if I was you.

PIERRE Um ... she's – she's not a wolf, she's – um ... a dog. (*He puts his hand gingerly on* LARA's *head.*) You tell him, Lara.

LARA (*trying to speak*) Grreeeggheeegghuuu.

MR PUNCH Looks like a wolf to me. You're taking quite a risk there.

LARA *shows the tips of her sharp teeth.* MR PUNCH *quickly steps back.*

MR PUNCH   You know what they say about
               wolves. Why, I heard a pack of
               wolves just ate an entire family!

PIERRE   (*bitterly*) I know all about wolves.
               You don't have to remind me. But –
               she's not a wolf. She's my friend.

PIERRE *puts an arm around* LARA's *neck. She peers up at him. If a dog can smile, she is smiling.*

PIERRE   She promised she wouldn't eat me.

MR PUNCH   (*unconvinced*) I see. A wolf's
               promise. Well, that's up to you,
               I suppose. (*Briskly*) Right, you
               were telling me where you were
               heading?

PIERRE   We're going to my—

LARA *grabs* PIERRE's *sleeve with her teeth.*

LARA   Grrrrrrrr!

MR PUNCH   Your grandmother's, eh? I can give you a lift, if you like. Just you, mind, not the, er ... (*he gestures at* LARA) ... dog.

PIERRE   (*frowning*) Did I tell you I was looking for my grandmother? I don't think I did. How did you know that?

MR PUNCH   (*airily*) I know a lot of things – especially about grandmothers! You'd be surprised. Come on then, hop on up.

PIERRE   (*to himself*) Could he really know where my grandmother lives?

LARA   (*fiercely, warning*) Grrrrrr!

LARA *crouches with her teeth bared, ready to pounce. Again the* OLD HORSE *stamps its feet.* PIERRE *is torn.* MR PUNCH *tries to catch him by the collar of his jacket. At that moment* LARA *springs, her claws glinting like knives.* MR PUNCH *lets out a screech and pulls out his club again. The* OLD HORSE *whinnies and rises on its back legs.* LARA *knocks* MR PUNCH *down to the ground. The lantern falls from the cart and goes out with a* phht *and the stage is in darkness.*

LARA (*her own voice returning*) Pierre! Quick! Jump into the cart!

LARA *throws herself onto the cart, and* PIERRE *scrambles after her. The* OLD HORSE *bolts away, the cart rumbling behind with* PIERRE *and* LARA *on board, wheels spinning at full speed down the winding path.*

SCENE TWO

THE EDGE OF THE FOREST

Enter the OLD HORSE, *pulling the cart with* LARA *and* PIERRE *in the back. They have come through the edge of the forest into open grassland. The* OLD HORSE *slows down and comes to a halt.* LARA *and* PIERRE *get down from the cart.*

LARA (*arching her back*) I'm glad that's over! What a journey!

PIERRE Me too. So many twists and turns!

The OLD HORSE *pulls the ramshackle cart over to the stream and lowers his head. He drinks deeply, slurp after slurp.*

LARA   I wonder where we are?

She puts her nose to the ground, sniffing.

PIERRE   (*puzzled*) Um, Lara, before ...
            you know, when that – that man
            was here – you didn't speak.
            You growled.

LARA   (*nodding*) Yes, it was so strange.
            I was trying to speak, and all that
            came out of my mouth was a growl.

The OLD HORSE *stops drinking.*

OLD HORSE   It was the same for me. I could only
            neigh and whinny when I was with
            him. Yet now, as you can hear, I can
            speak perfectly well.

LARA   That was a very bad man, Pierre.
            You shouldn't have been talking
            to him.

PIERRE   I know. I was silly. It was only
            that for a moment I thought –
            I thought—

OLD HORSE   (*coughs slightly*) I wonder if one of
            you wouldn't mind unhitching me
            from this silly cart?

PIERRE   Of course! I'm sorry. I can do that.

PIERRE *goes over and finds the place where the* OLD
HORSE *is attached with a chain and unlatches it. The
cart sinks down on its rickety wheels and then collapses
with a crash of wood and metal into the mud.*

OLD HORSE   Ahhh, that is a relief! (*He coughs
            again.*) I wonder, could you perhaps
            take off my reins, and the bridle?

LARA   I'll do it.

With her teeth she tears away the pieces of leather the OLD HORSE *is tangled up in, as well as the hoods that cover his eyes. He has wonderful eyes, like black pearls.*

OLD HORSE   Oh my! (*He scampers about like a puppy, through the grass, around in a circle and back again.*) Oh MY!

He stops cantering about and comes back to LARA *and* PIERRE.

OLD HORSE   I must thank you both for what you did back there, helping me escape from that wicked man. I am old and thin and not good for much, and I can't remember the last time anyone stood up for me. You did (*nodding at* PIERRE) and so did you (*nodding at* LARA).

LARA   (*embarrassed*) Well, it was you who did all the galloping away and for such a long distance. We are the ones who have to thank you.

PIERRE   (*stroking the* OLD HORSE's *muzzle*) I am so glad you got away from him.

OLD HORSE   (*nuzzling* PIERRE) To return the favour, how can I help you?

PIERRE   (*hopefully*) Can you help us?

LARA   Find Pierre's grandmother? Could you?

OLD HORSE   I can certainly try. Where does she live?

PIERRE   All I know is that she lives on the other side of the river.

OLD HORSE   Other side of the river ... mmmm. That *is* far ...

PIERRE (*sadly*) I know. I have been trying to get there for such a long time.

OLD HORSE Climb up on my back, and we'll do what we can. No wiggling, all right?

PIERRE (*delighted*) Thank you! That would be so much easier. (*He climbs up on the back of the* OLD HORSE.) Lara too?

OLD HORSE (*doubtfully*) If you're sure she's not a wolf ...

PIERRE She's not a wolf. Come on up, Lara!

LARA (*darting about*) I'm all right. I'd better stay here to keep the scent of the trail. (*Muttering to herself*) Grandmother, grandmother, grandmother.

OLD HORSE   (*whispers to* PIERRE) Are you quite sure she's *not* a wolf?

PIERRE   (*stoutly*) She's my friend.

OLD HORSE   Doubtless. Mmmm. Are you sure she knows what she's doing?

PIERRE   What do you mean?

OLD HORSE   Most of the dogs I know, when they are tracking someone – well, they have a clue from the person. You know, a piece of clothing, something like that. That's the way they track them down.

PIERRE   I don't have anything like that for my grandmother. Nothing at all. All I know is that she's on the other side of the river.

OLD HORSE   I see. Well, then, the best thing we can do is head off for the river, straightaway!

PIERRE   (*brave and bold*) Yes! To my grandmother's!

The OLD HORSE *whinnies, and then sets off at a trot, with* LARA *loping behind.*

SCENE THREE

AT THE FOOT OF THE MOUNTAIN

Enter LARA, *exhausted. She can hardly lift her feet. The* OLD HORSE, *equally slow and tired, carrying* PIERRE, *who is slumped on the* OLD HORSE's *neck, enters after her.*

LARA   How long we have been walking! Up and down, hill after hill. I'm so hungry! Always so hungry. And I keep imagining all sorts of delicious things to eat. (*She sits down on her haunches and closes her eyes dreamily.*)

> Toast and butter and honey and cream, yes, cream and scones with raisins and sultanas and ...

PIERRE *slides down from the* OLD HORSE's *back and comes and sits next to* LARA.

PIERRE   And jelly and ice cream, and rainbow cake and— (*He stops.*) Lara!

LARA   (*still dreaming*) What?

PIERRE   All that food you're talking about—

LARA   Mmmm?

PIERRE   That's not the sort of food a dog would eat, is it?

LARA   No ... maybe not ... (*She jumps up and gives herself a shake.*) Back to the important things.

	Where are we? Are we any closer to the river? (*She sniffs the ground.*)
PIERRE	(*hopefully*) Any ideas?
LARA	Not exactly.
OLD HORSE	(*to* PIERRE, *whispering*) I told you so. She's not experienced.
PIERRE	(*quick to panic*) What are we going to do?
LARA	I'm trying as hard as I can! Just give me a moment to think about it, will you? (*She stops sniffing, and throws her head back and starts to howl.*) Harooooooooooooooooooooooooo! Haroooooooooo!
PIERRE	(*his arms around her*) Don't cry, Lara!

LARA   (*indignantly*) I'm not crying! I'm just having a good howl. That's what we – er – dogs – do when we're thinking hard. (*She throws her head back again.*) Haroooooooooooooooo! Haroooooooooooo!

OLD HORSE   (*to himself*) Sure sounds like a wolf to me.

Out of nowhere, something comes flying through the air and lands with a thump in the middle of the stage. LARA stops howling, startled.

PIERRE   What on earth? (*He goes over to the object and picks it up.*) It's – it's a ball of wool!

LARA   Where did it come from?

PIERRE   I – I don't know.

The ball of wool jerks out of his hands and bounces across the ground. PIERRE *runs to pick it up again. It jerks out of his hands a second time. A red thread leading from the ball stretches right off the stage.*

LARA (*excited*) I think there's someone on the other end!

PIERRE The other end of what? You mean, over the mountain?

He picks up the ball of wool again and holds it very tightly this time. The thread tugs back.

OLD HORSE (*shaking his head*) Not *over* the mountain, my young friends. *Through* the mountain.

PIERRE How can that be?

OLD HORSE There's a tunnel. Right through the mountain. I've heard about it, many times. I never believed I would ever see it.

The OLD HORSE *shakes his head in wonder. The ball of wool jerks again, impatiently.*

LARA   Who – who could it be, on the other end?

OLD HORSE   I don't know. I don't know who lives over there. As I said, I've only ever heard about it. It could be anyone.

LARA   Well, there's only one way we will ever find out.

PIERRE, *holding the ball of wool in one hand, and with the other hand on* LARA's *back, moves to the dark gaping hole at the foot of the mountain. In trepidation, they head together offstage, the* OLD HORSE *trudging after them.*

SCENE FOUR

IN AND OUT OF THE TUNNEL

Enter PIERRE, LARA *and the* OLD HORSE. PIERRE *is clinging onto the red thread. It is pitch dark.*

PIERRE   (*shivering*) How cold it is in here!

LARA   (*glancing down*) And the ground is full of water. Icy water.

OLD HORSE   We're in the middle of the earth, my friends. You'd expect it to be cold. The sun never shines down here.

LARA   No ...

She opens her eyes wide. Out shoot two strong beams of white light, like two intense ghostly torches.

PIERRE   (*amazed*) Lara! How did you do that?

LARA   I – I don't know. But I did it.

OLD HORSE   (*under his breath*) Definitely a wolf.

LARA   At least we can see our way and how much further we've got to go.

LARA *shines the lights of her eyes up and down. The walls of the tunnel are wet and slippery with curling moss. There is the relentless sound of a drip, drip, drip of water from above.*

PIERRE   (*in despair*) We'll never get out of here! This tunnel is too long. We are going to be here forever and ever ... We're going to starve, or worse!

OLD HORSE (*calmly*) We won't starve, Pierre. We'll just keep going, you'll see.

PIERRE Just keep going?

OLD HORSE That's the way. Just keep going until—

PIERRE Until?

OLD HORSE Until you can't.

PIERRE (*in a small voice*) Until I can't.

LARA Pierre! Don't be like that. Don't give up. Remember there's someone at the end of the ball of wool. See – it's tugging right now! They want us to keep going.

The wool jerks back and forwards several times impatiently.

PIERRE   (*muttering*) Keep going, keep going, keep going ...

LARA   I'm sure we're nearly there, Pierre. I just know it.

She's right. Suddenly the stage bursts with blazing sunlight revealing a small girl in a floppy hat, ZADY. She is wearing a blue coat that trails on the floor like an oversized dressing-gown and has brown battered laced-up boots peeking out from under the coat's hem. She is holding the end of the red thread of wool in her fingers and is pulling on it, jumping up and down in excitement. She tugs and tugs until PIERRE tumbles right on top of her followed by LARA and the OLD HORSE.

ZADY   (*twirling around in joy*) At last! You're here!

LARA blinks several times. PIERRE stands dazed as if he can hardly believe he got out of the tunnel. The OLD HORSE heaves a huge sigh.

PIERRE   We're out! I can't believe it! We
                made it out of there!

LARA   Where are we? (*To* ZADY) And –
                who are you?

ZADY *seizes the ball of wool from* PIERRE's *hands.*

ZADY   (*triumphantly*) Everything has
                worked out exactly as I wished!

OLD HORSE   Hem, young lady, may I ask—

ZADY   (*running over to the* OLD HORSE)
                What a lovely old horse!

She strokes his mane.

LARA   What do you mean – exactly as
                you wished?

ZADY   (*skipping about*) It's wonderful,
                it's just so wonderful!

PIERRE   Please! Tell us what you are talking about!

ZADY   I will, I will. (*She rolls up the ball of wool.*) You see, I was sitting by myself knitting, which is what I do when I feel very sad, and I closed my eyes and I wished and wished for someone to help me. (*She beams.*) And my wish came true!

LARA   What wish?

ZADY   (*gazing at them all with her round green eyes and her huge unfailing smile*) The singing! I heard it all the way from the other side of the mountain!

PIERRE   Singing?

ZADY   (*in a swoon*) It was the most beautiful voice I've ever heard!

(ZADY *closes her eyes for a moment.*) Beautiful! So I did the only thing I could think of. I threw down my ball of wool, as hard as I could, right through the tunnel like a bowling ball, and then I wished that whoever was singing would catch hold of it and come through the mountain!

PIERRE (*apologetic*) Um, there's one problem. It was none of us that were singing.

ZADY (*face falling*) Wh–what?

PIERRE None of us were singing. I'm afraid you must have heard someone else.

OLD HORSE (*coming forwards, coughing*) Hem, I wonder if perhaps – perhaps she heard our young friend here (*he gestures at* LARA) um – howling?

ZADY	Howling? (*She stares at* LARA, *comes closer, really examining her, and then suddenly takes a step backwards in horror.*) You're a wolf!

LARA	No! I'm not a wolf!

ZADY	You're not?

LARA	No! I'm a dog!

ZADY	(*very uncertain*) A dog?

PIERRE	(*robustly, his arm on* LARA's *neck*) She's a dog. She really is a dog. (*Talking himself into it.*) She is definitely a dog.

ZADY	Well, you look just like a wolf. See for yourself – on this poster right here.

She points to a poster plastered on a wall behind them. There is a picture of a wolf with huge teeth and lines of big black words underneath.

PIERRE (*reading the poster aloud in a quavering voice*) 'WOLVES AT LARGE! BEWARE! ENTIRE FAMILY EATEN BY A PACK OF WOLVES! DO NOT APPROACH. CALL THE GUARDS AT ONCE!'

He turns slowly to LARA. *She wags her tail slightly, nervous.*

PIERRE She's not a wolf! She's a – she's a dog. She's my friend. She wouldn't eat anyone. Would you, Lara?

LARA (*firmly*) Never.

ZADY Hmmm. (*She keeps her distance from* LARA.) Anyway, it wasn't howling I heard. It was definitely singing.

WOLVES AT LARGE!

BEWARE!

[EN]TIRE FAMILY
[EA]TEN BY A PACK
OF WOLVES!

DO NOT
APPROACH

[C]ALL THE GUARDS
[A]T ONCE!

OLD HORSE	Perhaps if she shows you. Lara, go on, give us a howl. Like you did before. Go on.

LARA *shrugs her shoulders. She stands in the middle of the stage and throws her head back, her nose pointing up to the sky.*

LARA	Harooooooooooooooooooo! Haroooooooooo! HarooooooooooooooooOOOOOOO!

ZADY	(*transported with delight*) It *was* you! The singing was you! I've never heard anything like it! You have the most beautiful voice in the world!

LARA	If you say so.

ZADY	I know it will work, I know it will!

PIERRE	Um, *what* will work? What are you talking about?

ZADY   Ah. I forgot. You don't know.

OLD HORSE   (*patiently*) Why don't you tell us all about it?

ZADY   It's my dad, you see. He's asleep.

OLD HORSE   Mmm? We do all like a snooze from time to time.

ZADY   No, no! I mean he's *really* asleep! He went to bed one day and then never woke up. He has been asleep for years and years. Hundreds of years!

PIERRE   How can he have been asleep hundreds of years? You're only a little girl.

ZADY   (*frowning*) I know, I have wondered that too.

LARA   Have you tried to wake him up?

ZADY   I've tried EVERYTHING. You name it. Bells, buckets of water, banging pots and pans, drums, eleven thousand voices all shouting 'Happy Birthday'. He just turns over, snoring his head off. But your singing (*she turns to* LARA, *beseechingly*) is so beautiful, I know it will wake him. I know it will. As soon as I heard it, I knew it was the answer to my wish. Please come with me and sing for him! Please! It's not far! Please!

PIERRE   Wait a minute! (*He waves to the sign.*) Lara can't go anywhere – it's too dangerous! We know she's not a wolf, but if you thought she was, then other people might too.

ZADY (*downcast*) Yes, you're right. If people see her … (*Her voice trails away, then brightens.*) I know! If you stand up straight and put on my coat and hat, then nobody will know you're a wolf! Nobody will see your furry legs or your big ears. And if you keep your teeth out of sight, you will be perfectly safe!

Before LARA *can reply,* ZADY *takes off her long blue coat. Underneath she is wearing a silver dress with sparkling stars. Then she removes her hat. Woolly brown hair spills down her shoulders. On top of her head is a circle of gold, studded with jewels. She heaves* LARA *up on two legs and wraps her coat around* LARA's *shoulders, and squashes the floppy hat onto her head.* LARA's *front claws edge out of the bottom of the sleeves, and her back paws are almost completely hidden by the length of the dressing gown. Her face is lost under the floppy hat, except for the tip of her wet nose.*

PIERRE   Lara! You look so funny!

LARA   (*wrinkling her nose and wobbling*) I *feel* funny, all right. Are you sure about this?

OLD HORSE   Very ... pleasant. He-hem. Yes, very pleasant.

ZADY   (*clapping her hands*) She's perfect! Let's go to the palace!

LARA   (*growling, uncomfortable*) Wait a moment. Did you say palace?

ZADY   (*impatiently*) Yes, yes, that's where Dad lives.

PIERRE   Your father lives in a palace?

ZADY   Of course. He's the King, you see.

PIERRE	(*slowly*) The King! That's why, that hat on your head – it's a crown. You're a princess.
ZADY	(*with a mock curtsey*) Princess Zady, pleased to meet you. As you see, though, I prefer to cover myself up. People have such funny ideas about princesses.
LARA	(*pointing at* ZADY's *crown*) It's sewn onto your hair. The crown, I mean. I can see big black stitches.
PIERRE	Doesn't that hurt?
ZADY	(*touching it*) Not really. (*She shrugs.*) At least it never falls off. Anyway, will you come? To sing to my father? To wake him up? Please, will you come? Please?

PIERRE   Is it very far?

ZADY   Just a hop and a skip! In the heart of the city. You'll see.

LARA   A city?

ZADY   Yes, you'll see. Please, do hurry! I can't wait!

OLD HORSE The thing is, er, Princess Zady, we are on the way to this young man's grandmother's—

But ZADY *has already darted off stage with* LARA, *who is walking on two legs.* PIERRE *and the* OLD HORSE *glance at each other.* PIERRE *climbs on the back of the* OLD HORSE *and they exit after the others.*

SCENE FIVE

THE CITY STREETS

ZADY *leads* LARA, PIERRE *and the* OLD HORSE *helter-skelter, bouncing, bounding, tripping through the heart of a city. High buildings, tall trees, towers, gates, fountains, squares, markets, parks, rise up on either side of the road. The city is bursting with* PEOPLE *pelting in all directions, intent on all sorts of activities, buying and selling, sweeping and digging, painting and juggling.* PASSERS-BY *wave and raise their hats.*

SCENE SIX

INTO THE PALACE

ZADY, LARA, PIERRE *and the* OLD HORSE *arrive at the gates of the royal palace on one side of the stage. The curtains are half-drawn. Just visible behind the curtains is a building of domes and towers and spires covered in gold leaf and windows that sparkle like bright water. A starry flag flies on a flagpole, making the sound of a whip cracking in the wind. Below the flag are a line of* SOLDIERS *with spiked guns on their shoulders, marching up and down in a funny jagged way, like a dance.*

ZADY   We're here!

SOLDIERS   (*bowing low, speaking together*)
               Your highness.

ZADY   (*embarrassed*) Please don't do that.

The SOLDIERS *stand up straight.*

ZADY   I've brought someone to see my father, the King.

At the mention of the word 'king', the SOLDIERS *clap their legs together in attention. One puts a trumpet to his lips and blows it, one bangs a drum and another clashes a cymbal. The* SOLDIERS *fall into two lines to make a guard of honour.* PIERRE *slips down from the back of the* OLD HORSE. ZADY *leads the way through, followed by* LARA, PIERRE *and the* OLD HORSE.

ZADY   (*nodding at the* SOLDIERS)
               Thank you so much. Thank you.
               (*She hisses at* LARA) Keep on your hind legs, remember!

The curtain rises and the three friends enter the palace. The floor is made of dirt and leaves, and the walls are covered with spider webs. There are rows of stakes with live flames casting a wavy light in the darkness. There is also a big sign: **WOLVES AT LARGE! BEWARE! BEWARE!**

LARA (*shivering, pulling her coat more tightly around her, in a low voice to* PIERRE) Peculiar palace, if you ask me.

ZADY (*beckoning*) This way.

There is a rumbling through the room, like quiet thunder, like a kettle boiling over on a stove.

PIERRE Is that—?

ZADY That's Dad! That's him snoring. Come on.

ZADY brings them to a giant four-poster bed. It has a golden canopy and is toppled over with tasselled pillows and thick woollen blankets. An armed SOLDIER *stands to attention at each corner of the bed. The eyes of the* SOLDIERS *are black and still, staring straight ahead of them, as though they see nothing. On top of the high bed, lying on his side, with a golden crown studded with gems on his head, half-nestled in his great elbow and snoring loudly, lies a huge brown bear.*

PIERRE   (*mouth falling open*) But—

LARA   That's a bear!

ZADY   That's my dad, all right.

LARA   You mean to say your father is a *bear*?

ZADY   (*proudly*) A bear, and a king.

She leans over and kisses the BEAR-KING's *furry cheek. He rolls over, and pushes his big head on top of one of the pillows.*

BEAR-KING   SnOOOOOOOOOORrrrrrrrrrre.

ZADY   (*sighing*) You see how sound asleep he is? Nothing, nothing we have tried will wake him. I'm sure, though, if you would sing to him that beautiful song I heard you singing through the mountain, it will do the trick. (*She clasps* LARA's *front paw.*) You are my last hope ...

More SOLDIERS *enter the room, filing in silently from outside. They stand in several rows around the* BEAR-KING's *bed, all with rifles on their shoulders.*

LARA   Well ... I ... (*whispering to* PIERRE) What if it *doesn't* wake him up?

PIERRE   (*uneasily*) I think you'd better start singing, Lara. I don't think they'll let us leave if you don't.

LARA   Oh, all right. It feels a bit ridiculous though.

OLD HORSE   (*warily eying the assembled SOLDIERS*) There are worse things than being ridiculous.

LARA   Okay, then. Here goes.

LARA takes a deep breath, throws her head back and opens her jaw wide. All her white shiny teeth are quite visible.

LARA   **HaROOOOOOOOOOOOO! HaROOOOOOO! HaROOOOOOOOOOOOO!**

The howling reaches the roof of the palace and the notes bounce back down again, back and forth, from ceiling to floor, from wall to wall. The air is overwhelmed with the sound, like ocean waves rolling onto the shore and then back again into the deep unknown.

LARA **HaROOOOOOOOOOOOO!**
HaROOOOOOO!
HaROOOOOOOOOOOOO!

The room begins to fill not just with SOLDIERS *but all kinds of other* PEOPLE *too, some dressed in velvet and jewellery, others shoeless in rags, all drawn by the sound. Animals swarm in to listen*: DOGS, CATS, CHICKENS, GOATS, MONKEYS *and even* ELEPHANTS.

LARA (*refilling her lungs*)
HaROOOOOOOOOOOOO!
HaROOOOOOO!
HaROOOOOOOOOOOOO!

Her howling is deeper than a siren, like the song of a lonely travelling bird that has lost its flock and can't find its way home. One of the SOLDIERS *begins to cry. Big tears ooze out of his motionless eyes and slip down his cheeks. Soon everyone in the room is crying, rows and rows of weeping* SOLDIERS *and* EVERYONE ELSE, *including* PIERRE *and the* OLD HORSE, *sobbing into their handkerchiefs. The whole room is cocooned in tears. Only* ZADY *does not cry. Her eyes are intensely fixed on the* BEAR-KING.

ZADY   (*voice shaking*) I think – I think he's waking up ...

The room falls silent. EVERYONE *gazes at the* BEAR-KING. *He is drawing his big paws out from under the blankets. Then he kicks the blankets and cushions across the floor with one of his huge legs. A mysterious emotion spreads over his sleepy face.*

ZADY   (*gasping*) Ah!

The BEAR-KING *unsheathes his claws and bares his teeth. Then in one great movement he throws off all the bedclothes and stands upright, his legs like columns of an ancient building, his crown glinting on his head, his eyes flashing.*

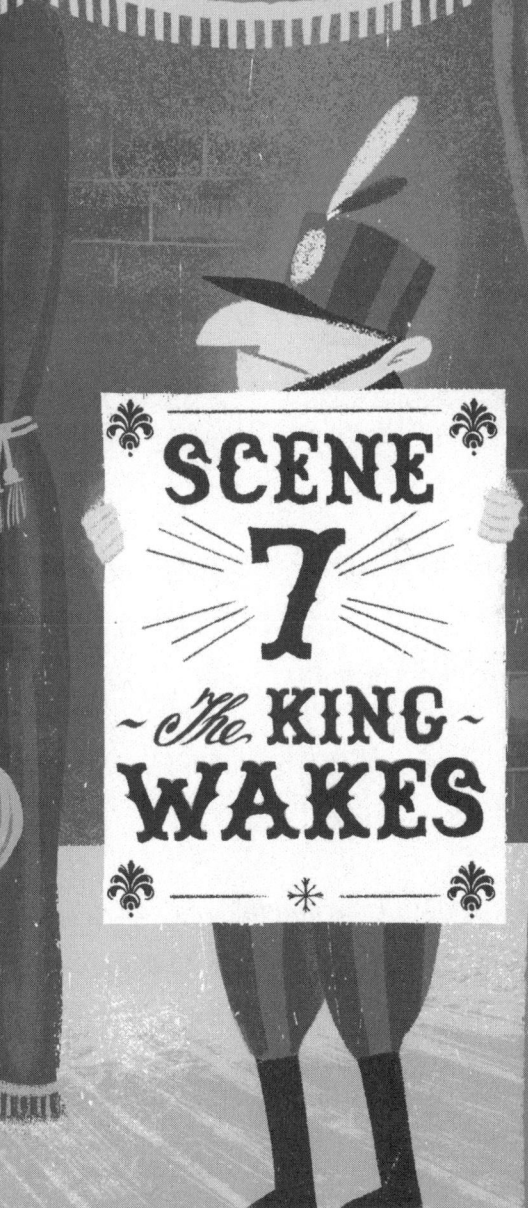

SCENE SEVEN

THE KING WAKES

The BEAR-KING *grins with a toothy smile that spreads from one furry ear to the other, and encloses* ZADY *in a deep bear hug.*

ZADY   (*muffled*) Daddy! You're awake at last!

BEAR-KING   (*murmuring and yawning*) Zady, Zady, little daughter, little daughter. What's all this? Have I been asleep?

ZADY (*accusingly*) You've been asleep for AGES! Centuries, actually. We've all been waiting SO LONG.

ZADY waves a hand at the throng that has gathered around, taking up all the space on stage.

BEAR-KING (*sheepish*) Have all these people been waiting for me? (*to* ZADY) Why on earth didn't you wake me up?

ZADY (*indignant*) I tried and tried and tried! I nearly EXPIRED trying. I tried EVERYTHING. And then at last—

She looks for LARA, *who is hiding nervously behind* PIERRE. *ZADY leans down and catches hold of* LARA's *front paw and draws her out so the BEAR-KING can see her.*

BEAR-KING (*perplexed*) Who's this?

ZADY   She's the – um – one who managed to wake you up at last!

BEAR-KING   You! You woke me? How did you manage it, er ... (*Smiling uncertainly at* LARA) ... young lady?

ZADY   It was her singing, Dad. She is the most beautiful singer. The MOST beautiful singer I had ever heard. I knew it would work.

BEAR-KING   (*nodding ponderously*) It's true that only the MOST beautiful singing would have the power to wake me.

LARA   (*from under her hat, modestly accepting the compliment*) Thank you, um, sire.

BEAR-KING   (*continuing*) Because there is NOTHING that I DETEST quite so much as beautiful music.

PIERRE (*astonished*) You don't like music?

ZADY (*laughing*) He hates music. HATES it. So that's why I knew you would wake him up. He would be so furious, you see!

The BEAR-KING *steps down from the royal bed into the middle of the floor. All the* SOLDIERS, PEOPLE *and* ANIMALS *bow and curtsey.*

BEAR-KING Not furious at all, my darling girl. I am overjoyed to be restored once more to the waking world. And now (*he lurches towards* LARA) for the ritual kingly bear hugs of supreme gratitude.

The BEAR-KING *hugs first* LARA, *then* PIERRE, *the* OLD HORSE *and* EVERYONE *in the room, one by one. He even hugs the coat rack and the lampshades.*

BEAR-KING   And ... oh dear.

He eyes a big official desk in the corner warily. There is a pile of papers on it reaching up almost to the roof.

BEAR-KING   (*glumly*) I see that I have a few Royal Notes to sign.

He puts his paw to his mouth and yawns.

ZADY   (*warningly*) Dad! You've only just woken up. You can't be tired already.

BEAR-KING   (*blinking*) Not tired exactly, darling. Although I must admit, when I see all the things I have to do, I can't help feeling a little drowsy. (*He stops and beams around at the crowd.*) I know! I think we must have a ball! A glorious waking-up ball!

(*He marches up and down, shouting.*) Bring out the long tables! Bring out the orchestra! Bring out the dance floor! And you ... (*He swings his paw around until it lands upon* LARA's *shoulder*) ... will be my Guest-of-Honour-in-Chief for your glorious services to the Kingdom!

LARA (*disconcerted*) Really, it's not necessary. I – I – don't know how to be a Guest-of-Honour-in-Chief!

BEAR-KING (*cheerfully*) And I don't know how to be a king! Still, we must all do the best we can with the melancholy tasks we are given. (*He claps his paws together.*) And now – on with the ball!

SCENE EIGHT

THE ROYAL BALLROOM

In an instant the whole room is lit up with chandeliers and spinning mirrors. Plaster grows along the walls like vines, in elaborate swirls and curls, and balloons, hundreds of green and red and yellow balloons fill the air above their heads. The dust on the floor is swept away to reveal shiny wooden boards and an orchestra appears complete with violins, trumpets and drums. Down from the ceiling a banner comes floating with the words: **THE KING AWAKES! REJOICE,**

REJOICE! *A gong rings out.* EVERYONE *shuffles backwards to make a space in the middle of the floor. The* BEAR-KING *emerges from the crowd, leading* LARA *by the foreleg into the centre of the room.*

BEAR-KING (*booming*) Behold, my Awakener! Please, everyone, your greatest applause!

There is an ear-splitting cheering and clapping and stamping of feet. LARA *and the* BEAR-KING *are standing next to two golden thrones. Right behind the thrones are the signs warning the public against wolves*: **WOLVES AT LARGE! BEWARE! BEWARE!**

PIERRE (*very anxiously to the* OLD HORSE) We must get Lara away from here! It's too dangerous for her. What if someone gets close and thinks she's a wolf?

OLD HORSE   (*his voice low*) I agree, Pierre. She can't stay here. How are we going to get her away, with all this going on?

BEAR-KING   (*with a flourish*) On with the noise! (*He addresses the* ORCHESTRA.) Nothing melodious, please. Just make a lot of banging and we'll all be happy.

The ORCHESTRA *strikes up a terrible crashing and screeching and the* BEAR-KING's *face is blissful. He sits on one of the thrones and gestures at* LARA *to sit on the other. Clearly nervous, she sits down next to him, glancing briefly up at the beware-of-the-wolf poster behind them. The* CROWD *begins to dance.*

BEAR-KING   (*loudly above the noise*) I hope you are enjoying the party?

LARA   (*her hat slipping to one side*) Er, well, yes—

BEAR-KING   (*peering*) My dear lady, may I say what remarkable eyes you have. Almost yellow.

LARA   (*quickly closing them*) Not really. Light brown. (*to herself*) I must get out of here. Where's Pierre? Where's the old horse?

One of the SOLDIERS *has grabbed* PIERRE's *arm and drawn him into a line of dancers, kicking and bowing and panting and running around and around, up and down in squares and frenzied circles. The* OLD HORSE *finds himself pushed up against the wall on the other side.* LARA's *hat partly slips from her head.*

BEAR-KING   My dear, I hope you don't mind my mentioning it, I can't help noticing, your ears are unusually large (*he quickly corrects*) yet perfectly charming, hem.

LARA   (*again, pulling the hat tight over her head*) It could be the weather, um, sire. I find it happens sometimes. (*Getting up from the throne.*) I think I really must be going. I must find my friends – I can't see them—

BEAR-KING   (*puzzled*) My dear, your teeth – may I say – I have never seen teeth quite so – so particularly (*he glances up at the poster behind the throne*) so extremely – so very—

LARA *is really panicking. She searches for* PIERRE *and the* OLD HORSE *in the dancing crowd. She only spots* ZADY *twirling around, her face growing redder and hotter.*

LARA   (*urgently, rising from the throne*) I really have to go. Thank you for the party, Your Highness – and good luck signing all those papers.

BEAR-KING   My dear—

In her desperation to get away, LARA *trips over the long coat that* ZADY *has lent her. There is a break in the crowd, and a figure rushes furiously forwards, coming to a halt in front of* LARA *and the* BEAR-KING.

MR PUNCH   (*violently*) STOP! Catch her! Stop her! She mustn't get away!

The ORCHESTRA *falls silent.*

BEAR-KING   (*bewildered, standing up*) What is this? What do you mean? What do you want?

MR PUNCH   (*pointing at* LARA) SHE – this so-called guest-of-honour – SHE – yes, SHE attacked me in the forest and left me for dead! She stole my property, my horse, my cart!

BEAR-KING   My dear fellow, how could you possibly say that this delightful, er, *unusual* ... young lady ...

MR PUNCH   (*with a cruel smile*) I will show you, I will show you all! You are giving a royal banquet in honour of (*tearing* LARA's *coat from her back*) a WOLF!

A huge gasp of horror rises like an icy breeze across the ballroom. LARA *stands very still for a moment, in shock. Then she throws the hat from her head and falls down on all fours, splendid and fierce, with her long matted fur, her thick tail, her claws, her ears pricked and her huge jaw and her wet wild eyes, ready to spring.*

SCENE NINE

CATCH THE WOLF!

A throbbing begins in the ballroom, a quiet drum at first, a train approaching, louder and louder, nearer and nearer, repeating over and over. Dozens of posters and banners appear and are raised on all sides:
WOLVES AT LARGE! BEWARE! BEWARE!

CROWD   A wolf! A wolf! A wolf! A wolf!

The ORCHESTRA *bangs their instruments in time, cymbals, drums, scratchy strings.*

CROWD   A wolf! A wolf! A wolf! A WOLF!

LARA *turns on the spot in a circle. She snarls.*

PERSON ONE   Look at her claws!

PERSON TWO   Look at her teeth!

PERSON THREE
            She will kill us all!

PERSON FOUR
            Catch her! Catch her!

EVERYONE   Catch her! Catch her! Catch her!

The SOLDIERS *hurtle forwards, surrounding* LARA *with their spiked guns, the same soldiers who only minutes before wept at the sound of her beautiful voice.* PIERRE *plunges into the crowd, trying to break through.*

PIERRE   Lara! I'm here!

SOLDIER ONE Keep back, boy! This is a wolf! Don't you know wolves are dangerous?

PIERRE (*angrily*) I know wolves are dangerous! Wolves ate my whole family! But I tell you she's not a wolf! She's a dog! (*through the barrier of* SOLDIERS, *solid as the iron stakes of a prison gate*) She's my friend! Tell them, Lara! Tell them you're not like those other wolves!

LARA *only growls deeply. Her claws are drawn.*

LARA Grrrrrrrrrrrrrrrrrrrrrrrrrrrrrrrrrrrr!

BEAR-KING (*holding his head*) I don't understand, I don't understand at all.

ZADY   (*pushing her way to the front*)
                  Stop them, Dad! Stop them!
                  Do something!

BEAR-KING   Zady, my daughter. I simply am at
                  a loss as to what is going on. This
                  lovely lady – my Awakener – my
                  Guest-of-Honour-in-Chief – all
                  this time, can it be true – all this
                  time she was – a wolf?

ZADY   (*sobbing*) It's my fault, Daddy!
                  I asked her to sing, to wake you up.
                  I knew her beautiful singing would
                  wake you up. And you're awake! It
                  worked! (*She clutches his paw.*) So
                  you must help her! Tell them to put
                  down their guns and let her go!

MR PUNCH   (*snapping*) Don't believe a word of
                  it, sire. The animal is a MENACE!

CROWD   Catch her! Catch her! Catch her! Catch the wolf!

The BEAR-KING *winces, and puts his big paws over his ears.*

BEAR-KING   This terrible shouting. All this arguing. Is this what I woke up for? I remember the world, it's all coming back to me – far too complicated and ugly. That's why I went to sleep in the first place. Soldiers! Bring me my bed!

Always obedient, the SOLDIERS *immediately bring the royal bed out from a corner. The* BEAR-KING *jumps onto it and buries himself under the blankets and pillows.*

ZADY   (*screeching*) Dad! Dad! Don't go to sleep! You can't! Wake up!

BEAR-KING Snoooooooooooooore ...
Snoooooooooooooore ...

CROWD (*in a chant*) Catch the wolf! Catch the wolf!

PIERRE (*desperate*) Zady – help us! Please!

ZADY I – I – don't know what to do! People here are afraid of wolves! Wolves do terrible things!

PIERRE Not Lara! Lara hasn't done anything!

The SOLDIERS *tie a rope around* LARA's *neck.*

SOLDIER ONE (*roughly*) Out of the way, boy.

PIERRE (*distraught*) Where are you taking her?

SOLDIER TWO We'll deal with her, don't you worry. We can't have wolves here. That's the law.

The SOLDIERS *pull on the rope around* LARA's *neck. She sits heavily on her haunches, resisting. They begin to haul her across the palace floor through the throng. The* CROWD *fall silent, watching the spectacle of the arrest.* PIERRE *tries to get to* LARA *but he is restrained harshly by the* SOLDIERS.

PIERRE (*his voice cracking*) Lara! Lara! My friend! Lara!

ZADY (*her head in her hands*) It's all my fault!

MR PUNCH (*cackling*) You will see what happens to wolves!

And then comes a tremendous sound, like a hundred boulders flying down a mountainside in an earthquake.

It is the OLD HORSE *flying from the back of the room like a warhorse.*

OLD HORSE   (*finding his voice and courage at last*)
NEVER!

He gallops powerfully towards LARA *and* PIERRE. *With a butt of the head, he dislodges the startled* SOLDIERS, *then in one swift bite of the rope frees* LARA.

OLD HORSE   **BOTH OF YOU! NOW! ON MY BACK!**

In an instant, LARA *and* PIERRE *clamber onto the* OLD HORSE's *back. The three friends take off at high speed in a thunderclap of hooves.*

The CURTAIN FALLS

Chapter NINE

The old horse galloped faster than he ever had before in his long, long, hard life. His heavy round hooves came down one after the other, on and on through the clouds of dust rising up about them.

Lara and Pierre hung onto his bony back, and clung onto his matted mane and each other, to stop themselves tumbling off. They galloped away from the palace, away from the shouting crowd and the shocked soldiers in pursuit. Lara was too frightened to look back. She could still feel the weight of the rope that had tightened around her neck.

Would the soldiers catch up with them?

But the old horse was fast and crafty. He took alleys and side streets; he cantered across parks and through the grounds of big buildings and the back lanes of houses. He changed direction, he turned in circles. On he galloped until there were fewer buildings, fewer houses, the shouting of the crowd faded to a whisper and then to nothing.

On they rode, on and on, until they were out of the city altogether. They passed great fields of wheat and sunflowers, farmhouses and windmills. Further and further and further ... The old horse kept going until at last one big hoof, then another, finally came to a stop.

Lara and Pierre slipped down from his back and fell face forwards onto a patch of soft grass. Nobody could move or speak. The terrible relief of escape left them feeling both very full and very empty at the same time.

Lara was the first to sit up. They were on the high mossy bank of a broad, winding river, which gleamed in the sunlight, blue and silver and shining purple. Wildflowers grew sloping down to the water, and blue and green butterflies bobbed about in the air, which smelled sweet, like pineapples. It felt like somewhere Lara had never known, full of ideas she didn't understand.

'We're free ...' she said, although she wasn't sure quite what she meant. 'We're free!'

'Yes,' said the horse, in such an old voice, like a horse that had lived for a thousand years. 'We are all of us free now,' and he bent down to chew on a nearby dandelion.

'Free,' repeated Pierre, glancing around, wondering.

Everything was quiet, except for a rocking of the water. Pierre lay down on his back, staring up at the sky. Lara stretched her furry legs. She lifted her nose in the air. She sniffed.

'Pierre,' she said, 'I think we are near your grandmother.'

Pierre stiffened. He gulped. 'How do you know?'

'I can feel it,' said Lara. Her ears twitched. 'In fact, I think that must be her house over there, across the riverbank.'

On the other side of the river there was a little house just peeping over the hill. It had mulberry bricks, a slate roof and white-framed windows. There was a chimney on one side of the roof and smoke – very fine, very pale – was rising out of it.

'Oh ...' breathed Pierre.

At the square window of the little house there was the shape of a person.

'Someone's at the window,' said Lara. 'She's waving at you, Pierre.'

The shape was waving a single hand, up and down, up and down, as though in the wind.

'Grandmother!' cried Pierre. 'It must be!' He bounded to his feet and hurled both hands above his head and shouted: 'Grandmother! Grandmother! It's me! It's Pierre!'

They were too far away to be heard. Yet the little figure at the window continued to wave.

'We must go there at once!' said Pierre.

'Yes,' agreed Lara. 'We have to cross the river. It's deep. I am a dog. I can swim. Can you, Pierre?'

'A little,' he said, faltering.

The water was so wide; it was more like an ocean than a river. Waves rippled and broke across the surface, twisted by the current. The old horse, who had wandered over to chew on some wildflowers, lifted his head and said: 'Friends, I have swum much further than that in my day. I am too old and tired to make the distance now. I have reached the end of where I can be, here, by this river, in this beautiful place.' He whinnied. 'You go, Pierre – you and Lara. She will help you cross. Go on, your grandmother is waiting.'

Pierre looked at the old horse and Lara, from one to the other and back again, and then across to the little mulberry-bricked house and the waving figure. His grandmother! His grandmother was there, waiting for him!

'He's right, Pierre,' said Lara, and there was no doubt in her voice. 'I can help you across. I will go first, and you come after me. You can hold onto me. We can get there together.'

'We can't leave you here,' said Pierre to the old horse, 'not after everything that has happened!'

'It is all right,' said the old horse kindly, nuzzling Pierre's shoulder. 'I am very happy here. In fact, I am happier here than I have ever been.'

Lara and Pierre both kissed the old horse goodbye at the soft spot on the top of his head. He smiled with all his teeth, which gleamed with laughter. *How young he seems*, thought Lara. She could see herself in the old horse's beautiful eyes, like two black mirrors. But – her face – was that—

'Off you go,' said the old horse. 'Help Pierre across the river.'

Pierre hung onto Lara's neck as they stepped down the slippery riverbank. The water's edge was thick with reeds. Lara put her feet in. The current was very strong.

'Follow me,' she said to Pierre, and she dived in and the river rose around her. 'Just hang onto me, if you feel you are sinking.'

She kicked her legs, pushing through the water. Tentatively at first, Pierre waded in after her. He grabbed onto Lara's fur and kicked. The old horse stood quietly on the riverbank, watching them, occasionally dipping down for another mouthful of grass.

Lara swam out into the powerfully rolling river, confident and swift, with Pierre in her trail. She felt the vibrations of her movement through the water like a motor. Pierre clung onto her, his head bobbing above the surface, yet she hardly felt him. It was as though she and Pierre were as weightless as clouds. Lara looked back for a moment, to see the old horse. But the whole river behind them was glowing with a golden fire and there was nothing more to see.

'Lara!' shouted Pierre in excitement. 'We are getting so close!'

He was right – they were nearly at the other side. The riverbed was thickening under her feet. She stopped swimming and began to trudge through the mud. Pierre, dripping wet and seized with energy, sprang up the riverbank ahead of her, lifting himself up with the reeds. Their sharp edges cut into his hands, but he didn't stop.

Behind him, Lara was slipping back into the mud. She felt herself sinking, then being sucked down.

'Pierre!' she cried. 'Wait!'

She was sinking deeper. She had become so heavy. The mud was wrapping itself around her. It was up to her neck.

Up on the riverbank, Pierre turned and saw Lara, disappearing. He lay himself down on the ground and stretched his hand as far as his arm could go. He lunged and then lunged again. Finally, he grabbed hold of Lara's paw. He tugged her out of the deep, by the toe, onto dry land.

Chapter TEN

'Pierre! Pierre!'

The door of the house behind the little hill flung open and a figure came running towards them, down the hill to the riverbank, her skirt billowing, her arms outstretched.

'Grandmother!'

Pierre ran to his grandmother. They threw their arms around each other, a tight bundle of happiness. Lara stood at a little distance, watching.

'Grandmother!' Pierre buried his face in her skirt. 'I wish I had something to bring you. Everything that was in our home is gone. I have to tell you—' He broke off.

'That's all right, little Pierre,' said his grandmother tenderly. 'We don't need anything. We have everything here.'

Pierre wiped his wet face. He looked up at her, confused.

'Why did you say "we", grandmother?'

His grandmother smiled and gestured at the house with the smoking chimney. In that moment all the windows and all the doors opened *crack, crack, crack, crack, crack, crack, crack!* and out jumped Pierre's seven brothers and sisters – and his mother and father! They all came running down the hill, their knees bouncing high in the air with their arms flying above their heads.

How could it be true? Pierre hugged them all, one by one, faint with joy.

'I thought I would never see you again!' he wept. 'I thought you had all been eaten up by the wolves!'

'We have been waiting here for you,' said his

grandmother. 'We knew you would come.'

A sweet breeze drifted above their heads. Pierre remembered Lara. Dear Lara.

'I have to introduce you to my friend,' he said to his grandmother.

He turned and reached out his hand to her. But—

'Lara?'

The Lara he had come to know was no longer there ... Her fur, her sharp teeth, her lolling tongue, all had gone.

'Lara ...' said Pierre.

A child stood upright in her place, in shorts and a shirt. She was wearing sandals on her feet. No paws.

'Lara – what's happened to you?'

Lara looked down at her own body, and then felt her own face with her fingers.

'I don't know,' she said. 'I don't understand.'

'Everything changes,' said Pierre's grandmother, 'when you come to the other side.' Her eyes shone blankly, like silver beads.

'Now you are your real self,' said Pierre's grandmother.

Real? Was she real? Even as the words entered her head, Lara felt a shadow falling. The seven brothers and sisters dancing around in circles lost their features; they were like pieces of paper being tossed in the wind. The little house became oddly flat, with a pale yellow light behind the windows. There was nothing behind it. It was empty. It was just paper and light.

She swung around. She was afraid.

'Pierre?'

Where was he? There was his mother and father, his grandmother, his seven brothers and sisters. In the twilight she couldn't make out their faces. They were all shadows, flying upwards. Which one was Pierre?

'Pierre!'

Everything was becoming dark. Above her head, she heard a bee buzzing.

Pierre! Pierre!
Pierre's not there!

Chapter ELEVEN

Buzzing and humming, buzzing and humming. Buzzing and humming.

Against a blocked-up fireplace, the dusty puppet theatre was propped at an angle. The red velvet curtains were frayed and old, and a pile of limp hand puppets were hanging over the edge of the stage.

Downstairs, Lara's mother was vacuuming. Lara sat listening – she didn't know for how long – until it stopped. Feet came up the carpeted stairs, thumping one after the other. The door of the room creaked. Her mother came in, taking a pair of gloves off her hands.

'There you are,' she said. 'Have you been here the whole time?'

The whole time, thought Lara. *The whole of time*. There were her feet. Her very own feet. And her arms, her fingers. She put a hand up to her face. There was her skin, her nose, her eyes, her ears. Her own hair.

'I thought you'd gone missing for a moment,' said her mother, walking into the middle of the room. She cocked her head. 'What's that buzzing sound?'

A little glass jar sat on the mantelpiece, reflected in a discoloured smoky mirror.

'It's a bee!' said Lara's mother. 'Poor thing. It's trapped.'

She picked up the jar. A bee was struggling inside it, knocking itself against the glass wall. Lara's mother took it to the window and thrust it upside down into the air.

The bee flew away, into the blue sunlight.

'That's better,' she said, closing the window with a firm bang.

Lara was thinking hard. She asked: 'Mum, do children live here? In this house?'

'No,' said her mother. 'No children. Are you wondering about the toys?' She pointed at the puppet theatre. 'That belonged to the man who owns the house, when he was a little boy.'

Lara wanted to say one word. *Pierre*.

'He told me he was given it by his grandmother,' said Lara's mother. 'He had a sad life, as a child. He lost all his family in the war, you see.'

Pierre, Pierre, Pierre's not there.

'Mum,' said Lara. 'What's his first name? The man who owns the house?'

'His first name?' Lara's mother put her hand on her hip. 'It's French. Pierre.'

She knew it, of course. Pierre. That boy was Pierre. She didn't know how it had all happened. She didn't know why. She put a hand up and touched the edge of the faded puppet theatre. Her fingers tingled.

It's magic, that's all. Magic.

'Anyway, I've finished, so we can leave,' said her mother. 'Let's head down to the water and have our picnic.'

Lara followed her mother down the stairs, into the hallway, then out the front door and down the stone steps. Two legs, not four. She waited while her mother locked up the door, with a firm click, and then hid the key again, in the little blue jar nestled in the rosebush.

The sun was high in the sky and they could smell the ocean rising, and they could hear the waves and the blast of the ferry horn, several long notes in a row, as it came towards the wharf.

'Let's take our time,' said her mother. 'We can catch the next one, or the one after that. And I want to make sure we get ourselves an ice cream before we go home.'

The park that led down to the water was overflowing with people, joggers, strollers, couples in one another's arms, kite flyers. Someone strummed a guitar under a tree near to where a group of children were playing French cricket.

Lara and her mother walked arm in arm past everything down to the little beach, a strip of sand next to the wharf. Further out to sea, the waves were huge and billowing, but here they lapped lightly, just wetting the pale yellow shore. As her mother laid out the picnic things, Lara went down to the water's edge. She took off her sandals and stepped in.

These are real things, she thought, staring

downwards through the bending waves. *Water, sand, wind, clouds, sky, air.*

She took a deep breath and then another. She curved her feet over the grit of broken shells, as the Pacific Ocean washed over them.

But there's magic too, she thought. *Everywhere.*

And she saw that on her toe, where Pierre's hand had pulled her out of the cold grasping river such a short – such a long – time ago, instead of a toenail was a little silver claw.

And back where the children were playing cricket, a big shaggy black dog lolloped playfully, wagging its tail, trying to catch the ball.

WHO'S THERE?

I've wanted to write a story about a puppet play for such a long time. When I was a child I loved putting on puppet plays at home, hiding behind the sofa or chest of drawers as a stage. I made puppets out of papier-mâché, I painted the scenery and wrote plays and songs, sometimes based on stories I loved. I remember especially my brother and I doing an epic version of *The Hobbit*. The only audience was the family, but we charged a 5-cent entrance fee, gave them tickets and handed out lollies at interval! (Yes, we even had an interval.)

I always had a secret wish though – that I could actually become one of the puppets and join in the play myself.

One day, many years later, when I was grown-up, I had a strange experience. I was on a tour of the famous royal Palace of Versailles in France, when I saw an open door of a building that seemed all locked up. I went in, not really knowing where I was going.

Inside it was very dark and mysterious. I walked forwards with slow steps, feeling my way. On either side of me, glinting in the dark, were rows of painted panels, lined up one against the other. I had such a fierce feeling of wonder, stronger than I have ever felt before. Where was I?

Suddenly from somewhere a voice called out: 'Who's there?' and a light came on. I blinked. I was in the middle of a stage! In front of me were banks of velvet chairs and everything seemed covered with gold. The person who had called out came up onto the stage and asked me what I was doing there. He told me this was a very special little theatre that had been built for Queen Marie Antoinette. Those painted panels were the scenery, from hundreds of years ago. But just for now 'The Queen's Theatre' was closed to the public. I said I was sorry, and backed out at once, out the door into the sunshine.

The whole experience in the little theatre only lasted a minute. But I think for that short, wildly exciting moment as I stood there in the darkness, I had just a glimpse of the feeling that Lara must have had when she found herself becoming part of a real puppet show ...

Ursula Dubosarsky was born and grew up in Sydney and wanted to be a writer from the age of six. She is now the author of over 60 books for children and young adults and her work is published all over the world. She has won several national literary awards and internationally she has been nominated for both the Hans Christian Andersen award and the Astrid Lindgren prize. Her most recent novel for children, *Brindabella*, was short-listed for the 2019 CBCA Awards. Ursula Dubosarsky is the 2020-2021 Australian Children's Laureate.

Christopher Nielsen is an award-winning Sydney-based illustrator specialising in children's books, advertising and packaging. His artwork is inspired by a passion for mid-century design, and has been short-listed for the CBCA Crichton Award and acknowledged by The British Book Design and Publication Awards, AGDA Awards, 3x3 Awards, Communication Arts, American Illustration and Society of Illustrators NY. He has received Gold, Silver and Bronze medals in the Illustrators Australia Awards.

SHORT-LISTED
CBCA Book of the Year, Younger Readers
Speech Pathology Awards, Eight to Ten Years
ABDA Awards, Best Designed Children's Fiction Book

This is a story about a boy called Pender and a kangaroo called Brindabella, about how they became friends, and all the things that happened to them because of it.

Pender and his father live in an old house made of honey-coloured stone in the bush by the river, with only the company of his father's paintings and the loyal dog, Billy-Bob. Then, on one winter morning, a gunshot amongst the trees changes everything.

When Pender rescues Brindabella from the pouch of her dead mother, an unusual friendship blossoms between the lonely boy and the orphaned joey. But Brindabella is no ordinary kangaroo. And though Pender has saved her life, the untameable wildness of the bush – and freedom – call to her ...

Lyrical and unforgettable, *Brindabella* explores the fierce beauty of the Australian bush.